To lovely Lola, Dolma and Ross

Scholastic Children's Books
Euston House, 24 Eversholt Street
London NW1 1DB
a division of Scholastic Ltd
London ~ New York ~ Toronto ~ Sydney ~ Auckland
Mexico City ~ New Delhi ~ Hong Kong

First published in hardback in the UK by Scholastic Ltd, 2005
First published in paperback in the UK by Scholastic Ltd, 2005
This paperback edition published in the UK by Scholastic Ltd, 2006

Copyright © Catherine Väse, 2005

10 digit ISBN 0 439 96847 X

13 digit ISBN 978 0439 96847 8

All rights reserved

Printed in Singapore

2 4 6 8 10 9 7 5 3 1

The right of Catherine Väse to be identified as the author and illustrator
of this work has been asserted by her in accordance with
the Copyright, Designs and Patents Act, 1988.

The Penguin who Wanted to Fly

by
Catherine Vāse

Hippo

Flip-Flop sat on his favourite thinking rock and looked up into the sky.

"I wish I could fly," he said to himself.

Flip-Flop stood up. He looked down
at his wings and flapped them.
Nothing happened.
Flip-Flop couldn't fly.

That night Flip-Flop had a dream.
He dreamt he was flying.
It was so quiet and so peaceful up there
in the starry sky.

Next morning Flip-Flop had
an idea. He would make
himself some wings.

"Can I help?" asked Polar Bear.

Flip-Flop climbed on top of
Polar Bear and flapped his wings.
FLIP FLAP . . .

FLOP!

"OOPS!" said Flip-Flop.
But it didn't matter.
Flip-Flop had another idea.

"Just the thing," said Flip-Flop as he pulled out his special helicopter hat from his dressing-up trunk.

He spun around and around and around and around and around and around, spinning faster, spinning faster and faster and faster...

until he spun out of control.
"Ouch!" cried Flip-Flop as he flopped
to the ground. "I feel very dizzy."

That night it snowed.
In the morning Flip-Flop was very excited
as he had thought of another idea.

He would build an aeroplane
out of snow, a snow plane!

Flip-Flop was very pleased with
himself as he climbed in.

5,4,3,2,1...

He waited for his snow plane to take off . . .
and waited . . . and waited.

"Oh dear!" sighed Flip-Flop
as the sun came out and melted
his snow plane.

But it didn't matter.
Flip-Flop had another idea, a better idea.

He got a balloon and tied
a piece of string to it.

The balloon floated upwards,
and so did Flip-Flop!

"I'm flying,"
said Flip-Flop excitedly.
"I am really flying!"
And so he was, until . . .

POP! went the balloon.

FLOP!
went Flip-Flop.
Poor Flip-Flop!

"I am never going to fly," he cried.

Polar Bear gave his friend a hug.
"Come with me," he said.

Polar Bear gave Flip-Flop a gentle push
down their favourite slippyslide.

WHOOSH!

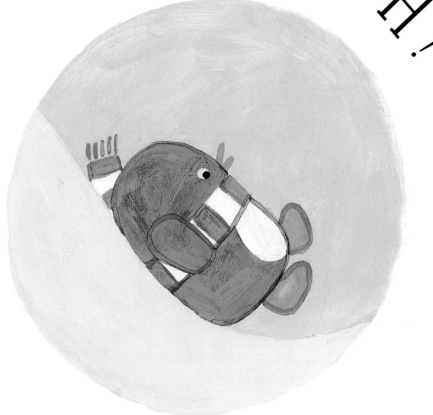

Flip-Flop whizzed down the ice.

"Wee-ee-ee, I'm flying!" squealed Flip-Flop.

But then . . .

"Help!" cried Flip-Flop as he crashed into the sea.

It was very peaceful and quiet down there under the sea. There were lots of fish and other floaty things.

"Wow!" said Flip-Flop. "This is just like flying!"

Flip-Flop couldn't really fly.

But that didn't matter, because Flip-Flop could swim.

In fact, he could swim quite beautifully.

The Penguin who Wanted to Fly